I0683759

Returning the Favor
and other slices of life

By John Hartness

Falstaff Books
Charlotte, NC
2009

For information on readings, or other nonsense
Visit me at http://www.johnhartness.com

Dedication

I couldn't have done this without the love and support of three incredible women:

My Mother, Frances Hartness, my inspiration

My Sister, Bonnie Alexander, my biggest fan

And most importantly

My Wife, Suzy, the best partner I ever dreamed of

Thank You.

Introduction

This collection of stories and poems is culled from fifteen years of my writing, all the way back to my early college years. Some of these have seen the light of day on my blog, some have been published in the internet literary magazine *Truckin'*, and some are seeing the light of day for the first time right here. I hope you enjoy them. Some of this is fiction, some is fact, and sometimes I can remember the difference. But I don't make any promises.

There are a few people I have to thank in addition to the three amazing women this book is dedicated to. I had some incredible teachers over the years, and I owe them a debt I can never repay: Deborah Hobbs, Kay McSpadden, Blair Beasley, Max Childers, Marc Powers, Anne Fletcher, Susan Ludvigson and Billie Hicklin are just a few.

I've also been fortunate enough to make friends with some great writers, and Paul McGuire and Brad Willis are the best of the best. These guys inspire me to take more chances, live harder and not to pull punches when I write it down.

So thanks for stopping by, I appreciate it. Kick off your shoes, grab a cold one and put some good music on. Oh yeah, one more thing – poetry should be read aloud. Always.

Vampire Poetry

I composed a great poem once at 3:14 AM in that
hazy type of half-asleep-yet-not-quite-half-awake
that only comes in the wee hours of the morning with
something asinine on the stereo as a futile insomnia
cure.

But I forgot it. And in the morning when I reached
for it in my head,
It was gone, somewhere hiding with that one missing
sock.

Like virginity and baby teeth, never coming back.

Moonlight

You wrap the night around me like a blanket
and we fall in love again
while the honeysuckle blooms
explode in my nose.
The rushing water in the distance
beats out a rhythm disjointed
from your even-uneven panting.
I can hear the sweat falling from your lips
when you kiss me
your hair falling over my face like a curtain
hiding us from prying lightning-bug eyes.
The grass beneath my back smells sweet as we
crush it into verdant Rorshach patterns
while we dance conjoined under the light
of a new moon and a hundred thousand stars.

Returning the Favor

I saw her sitting there, at the only patio table with an open seat. Sitting alone listening to her iPod on a gorgeous spring morning. One of those sparkling mornings that's just cold enough to carry a sweater, with just enough warmth in its smile to promise you won't need it.

"May I?"

"I...ok, sure." She gave the patio the once-over to see if there was another option, then gave me the required polite response when she saw it was either sit with her, or juggle my latte, muffin and novel while standing.

"What are you listening to?" I could see she was upset, and probably didn't want to talk, but I had a feeling it might be worth it to pry.

"I...it's a new Alanis Morrisette song. Her new album is all acoustic." I loved the way she paused for a second before answering, just that slightest hesitation when she wanted to tell me to piss off, but couldn't quite bring herself to do it.

I reach over, take hold of the dangling earbud, and pop it in. "You Oughta Know" sounds so different with a live drummer and acoustic guitar, but it still transports me.

Scent is supposed to be the sense most closely tied to memory, but for me it's hearing. A song can take me almost physically back to a moment in time, and this one was no different. It was almost 10 years ago, the album was new, Alanis wasn't a superstar yet, just another angry young chick carrying the Ani DiFranco banner for the next generation. And I was twenty, bleached blonde and jilted with her hit single blasting through my dorm room as I threw all of the sorry bastard's pictures, CDs and clothes out the window onto his head, drowning out his protestations and apologies with projectiles and expletives. He at least had the wisdom to run when I showed up in the window holding his guitar. He must have known the amp was coming next.

Annie, my roommate, opened the door, peeked in at the carnage, and swiftly decided that this would be a good night to study at the library. I spent another hour or so playing the raving Medea then decided I needed to be at home. So I abandoned the wreckage of my room, leaving an apocalypse of shattered glass and plastic on the sidewalk and the oak outside my window garlanded with t-shirts and sweaters. Two hours' drive later, I pulled up in front of my parents' house deep in the middle of the night. My kid sister, just fifteen, was sitting on the porch swing when I got out of my much-abused Cabriolet.

"Hey."

"Hey." I sat down next to her on the swing. We sat there for somewhere between twenty seconds and an hour; swinging on the porch, listening to the crickets and big rigs on the highway. Just sitting and swinging. I didn't need to talk, I just needed to be with somebody I still trusted.

"He fucked my best friend."

"I know. Annie called. She thought you might come home."

"He's a fucking piece of shit."

"Yep."

"I still love him."

"Yep."

And I curled up into a little ball on that swing, and my kid sister held me while I cried myself to sleep. I woke up the next morning in that swing with a blanket, a pillow and her stuffed monkey tucked under my arm.

A blaring horn jolted me back to the present and I caught the girl looking at me strangely. "I know this tune," I said.

"Yeah, the song's old. But the album's cool."

"Yep."

We sat there for a time without time, listening to Alanis on shared earbuds, until I reached out and touched her hand.

"You know he's not worth it, right?"

"Yep."

"Doesn't matter, does it?"

"Nope."

Then I reached into my bag, handed her the monkey, and held my little sister while she cried her soul out on the Starbucks patio.

Hollydays

Colbie Callait's singing Mistletoe on the XM holiday
station
While a little Mexican boy sits cross-legged
On his brown front yard
Looking down the street expectantly,
Searching traffic for a Greyhound sleigh
to bring Poppi home.

Two fat women,
One white with a bad dye job and a
Trailer-park linoleum kitchen hair style,
One black with a Santa hat and a wifebeater
Walk side by side along a busy street
Hauling their Wal-Mart groceries
And government cheese
Home
To the efficiency apartment with the Toys-for-Tots
gifts
And Methodist-donated decorations.

All the flowers in the cemetery
Are fresh
Except one.
What happened to you,
Mr. Robert Keziah 1953-2009?
Was he the last
Is he forgotten
Does nobody care
Is everybody busy

Why not him?

I like to walk among my ghosts
On holidays
It reminds me where I'm from.

The concrete angels
Watch over me
As I look at my name
Repeated
Over
And over
And over
All along the row with my
Uncles
Aunts
Cousins.

I look over my history
My family
My future?
While I steal a flower
Here
And
There
For Mr. Robert Keziah 1953-2009.

I won't tell if you won't, Bob.
They won't miss 'em
And maybe somewhere
It makes you smile.

Grits

It was my friend Melinda's birthday and we were in Birmingham, Alabama. That right there should tell you that this will not end well. We start our night at Dreamland, a legendary rib joint with the face of a smiling pig painted nine feet high on the side of the building. I'm always puzzled at the desire of barbeque restaurants to make you feel like you're dining on a Looney Tunes star, but the smiling pig picture has kept legions of sign painters in business for eons through the south.

So we get a table for twelve, and the waitress who seats us obviously knows how to deal with rowdy convention-going dorks like us.

"Y'all want beer or tea?" Remember this is Alabama; there is no question to the sugar content of said tea.

In chorus, a dozen theatre lighting salespeople harmonize the holy chorus of "Bee-eee-eeeeeee-eee-rrrrr!"

"Y'all want chicken or ribs?" I've never seen the word "chicken" *sneered* before, but I swear that's what she did. This lovely woman, Alabama's own answer to George Jefferson's Florence, with (I swear) an Aunt Jemima-red bandana on her head, actually *sneered* the word "chicken."

"Ribs. Lots." This from Alan, Melinda's boss, who had very fastidiously tucked his napkin into his necktie in preparation for the splatterfest that was soon to ensue. We did suggest that he might consider removing his jacket for the feast, but he assured us that he was a trained professional, perfectly capable of making it through a meal without wearing any sauce on his sleeve. In other words, this was *not* his first barbeque.

About 16 seconds later, Florence comes back with twelve beers, emerging from various pockets and apron receptacles like clowns from a VW bug, deposits two rolls of Bounty paper towels on the table, and two loaves of Wonder Bread.

The sad thing was, not a soul at the table even thought to ask "what's the bread for?" Every single, solitary person seated there immediately understood that not only was the bread going to be a far more effective napkin than anything else, but without bread, there can be no sopping. And with any good meal, the sopping is the best part, obviating any requirement for dessert or after-dinner drinks (although there would be plenty of after-dinner drinking).

About 47 consumed beers later (about 28 minutes in real time, but we were drunks on a mission), we had consumed everything but a local microbrew called Iron City Beer, and there were three aluminum foil roasting pans in the center of the table, playing host to enough ribs to create a $1/8^{th}$ scale model of the Capitol Dome. If you ever are in Birmingham and get the opportunity to try Iron City Beer, haul ass to the Mississippi line as quickly as possible.

After decimating the ribs and making short work of both loaves of soppin' bread, we decided that it was time to DANCE! This serves as an acceptable indicator of the higher level thinking that a dozen adults with about 19 degrees between them can engage in after consuming roughly their body weight in beer and ribs. This was not going to be pretty. It got less pretty when we found the nearest dance club, a charming place called Bell Bottoms. All disco, all the time. And me without my white suit. But it was Melinda's birthday, and she wanted dancing, so a-dancing we went.

Immediately upon entering the bar we were confronted with the sight of the inimitable Randy K and thirteen kamikaze shots. Walt two-fisted, because, well, somebody had to drink the last one. Several hours worth of dancing, drinking and Twister ensued (no Crisco was harmed in the playing of this Twister game), finally culminating in the removal of neckties, the blowing of kisses, the sprawling on floors and the closing down of the bar for the night. Salespeople in their barbeque-splattered convention clothes are less than appealing at 2:30 AM when the ugly lights come on.

But since it had been 6 hours and about 137 alcoholic beverages since we all last ate, we decided that a Waffle House run was mandatory. Now, let's look past for the moment the fact that Waffle Houses are somewhat frightening before midnight. Even when you're sober. But when you're drunk, fearless and hungry, you'll go places where no Yankee has ever gone before, like the Birmingham Waffle House at 3AM. And trust me, in Birmingham, my North

Carolina address marks me as a Yankee sure as if my last name was Sherman.

There might have been a few wrong turns to get us to the Waffle House. This might have been assisted by the fact that we had no directions and no one in the car was sober. Or had ever been to Birmingham before. There may have been an incident where we made a Secret Service level reverse-and-peel-out change of direction when we noticed a field sobriety checkpoint up ahead (as Walt hung out the rear passenger window yelling "Here, piggy, piggy, piggy" while we ran like West Virginia virgins). But finally, up ahead, was the welcoming golden glow that told me all would soon be well with the universe, the familiar yellow squares with one burnt out letter.

We took our seats at the bar and placed out order. In my best amazingly drunken Elwood Blues impression, I ordered 8 slices of white toast, two orders of bacon, and a chicken breast. Plain. Melinda had a waffle, which I'd never actually seen anyone eat at a Waffle House before, so it struck me as odd. And Walt ordered a monstrous breakfast with eggs, a double order of grits, bacon, sausage, toast and black coffee. I became very concerned with the upholstery on the ride back.

As our food arrived, two members of Birmingham's finest walked into the diner, looking for all the world like they really needed to find some drunken out-of-towners to lynch before they got off their shift at sunrise to return to their coffins. They walked the entire length of the bar, paused behind each one of us as we tried our best to sit upright, and sat down on the stool right next to Walt just as our food arrived. BubbaCop #1 ordered, asked Walt to pass the napkins, and as he turned around after giving BC the napkins, all the stress, strain and Kamikaze's of the night finally caught up with Walt. He took a good look at the cop sitting next to him; his face took on an expression of the deepest thought, and then morphed into utter calm as he finally passed out, facedown, right into his double order of grits, extra butter.

The cop and I looked at each other over Walt's slumped shoulders, shrugged in unison, pulled him back into an upright position, and ate our meals, one hand on each of Walt's shoulders while he snored little grit snores in the middle of the Waffle House.

Road Blues

Another lumpy hotel bed,
another meal alone.
Another town, another state
another night wondering what you're doing while I'm
gone.
I'm rolling west,
you're staying put.
I'm riding fast,
you're standing still.
I'm missing you,
you're standing on the porch watching me go.
Again.
I'm looking through my rearview mirror, hoping to
catch
another glimpse of you,
turning to look for me,
but you're gone.
I'm the one leaving,
but you're the one that's gone.
You're on the porch,
our porch,
watching me kick up a cloud of dust at the end of the
drive,
I don't know where I'm going,
but I know I'm chasing you.
I'm driving while
you're standing still,
but I'm the one chasing you.

Not just a river in Egypt

I never think of you anymore,
'til I see a picture of us some asshole put on
Facebook,
standing on the steps in front of my college dorm
decked out in our finest freakwear to go out on the
town,
nineteen and smiling like we've got our whole lives
in front of us,
or something stupid like that.

I never even notice we're not together anymore,
until I hear a song on my iPod
that you just had to had to haaaad to have
right
that
minute
so I got out of my very warm and comfortable bed,
thankyou*very*damnmuch,
and bought the MP3 for you off Amazon so you
could play it
seventeen times
at least
that night before you fell asleep
with your head on my shoulder
and your hair tickling my nose.

I never turn my head when I think I hear your voice,
unless maybe it's at that Starbucks on 7th St.
where we almost got thrown out
for being just a little too friendly
on the couches which just happened to be
in front of the windows

and there might have been a complaint from a mother or three
walking her kid to the comic book shop next door.

I never, EVER, don't go somewhere just in case you might be there,
except for what used to be our grocery store,
or VisArt,
or that Cajun joint in NoDa
with the bread pudding you used to love.
I guess you
probably
still love that bread pudding.

I never miss you at all hardly,
except at night.
nights are a little tough, I'll admit,
when there's not anybody
snoring so gently beside me
nobody hogging the blanket
and putting cold feet between my legs
just as I'm about to fall asleep
then giggling and kissing me breathless
before looking up at me with those kitten eyes and asking
"But you love, me, right?"

So I'm fine. Really, I don't ever really think about you.
Much. To speak of.
Anymore.
Really.

A Matter of Perception

Do you have any idea what this is talking about?

I looked to the left, and hanging out in midair beside my chair, was a brain. I knew it unmistakably as my brain, because it had my eyes. None of the rest of the things that comprise a face, or even a head, just a brain floating in midair with my eyes in front. I was only a little surprised to see it there, and that might have been part of the problem.

There may have been drinking involved. Actually, there was *definitely* drinking involved, but no alcohol. We couldn't afford it. Not even the 18-pack for $6 Milwaukee's Beast from the gas station on the corner. Underage was beside the point, underfunded was the obstacle. So we went to the next resort – acid. Nothing. Couldn't find a tab on campus at all for less than $10, a friggin' travesty given the quality we had been experiencing – that shit should have definitely been in the drug dealer's equivalent of a dollar store.

So the last resort sent us jaywalking across the less-than-busy four-lane road that was the main drag in Rock Hill, SC to the grocery store nearest campus. We knew the route well enough to have walked it blindfolded – in the front door, turn left, 10 steps, halfway down the aisle, middle shelf – Tussin DM.

You wanna talk about white trash hallucinogens, you can't really go any further into the trailer park than chuggin' a whole bottle of cough syrup with a Dr. Pepper chaser at 1PM on a Tuesday. So there was me & Chris, swaying a little at the foulness we'd just ingested, trying not to puke, and failing miserably. Didn't matter, even with the puke, a whole bottle of Tussin was still good for about seven hours of seriously bent reality.

So what do two 18-year-old kids gakked outta their minds on cough syrup do on a winter's afternoon? Go to the mall and look at the pretty lights, of course. Now we weren't satisfied with the local Trasheria Mall in Rock Hill. Oh no, we had to put the rubber to the road on the interstate and truck it up to the big two-story mall in Charlotte. Great idea. I'm sure there was driving, but my next recollection is looking at all the cooooooollllllll shit in the Everything's A Dollar store in the mall, then I see the really neat texture on the wall. Cool fleckstone paint always deserves a closer look, right?

This is when I remembered one of the great truths of physics – matter isn't really solid. I know this is true, because I learned it from X-Men comics when I was a kid, Chris Claremont would never lie, right (okay, excepting that whole Siege Perilous thing, which just sucked)We all know that there are really far greater spaces between atoms in a wall than appear to the naked eye, so at 1:47 PM on a Tuesday afternoon in 1992, I could see the precise molecular alignment of not just the wall of the Dollar Store, but also of *my hand.* I had found how to pass through solid matter, and it was time to try it out, right now!

I slowly extended my arm towards the wall, being very careful not to move to quickly, lest I misalign my molecules with those of the wall. Closer, less than a foot from the wall, I can see everything lining up for me to be able to reach through the wall and wave at Chris from outside while part of me stays inside. Closer, six inches from the wall, moving, moving,

"Hey, you okay over there?"

SLAM – the bright lights of the mall go off like sirens in my head screaming "They all know you're fucked up! Act straight! Act like you're not tripping daisies!"

"Dude, he just got out of the hospital, leave him alone" Chris to my rescue. And we bolt, giggling like 8-year old girls (albeit really, really fucked up 8-year old girls). And as we settle into the car for the return trip to campus, I look over at Chris with a look of absolute terror on my face.

"Dude, what if he'd done that while my hand was in the wall?"

pause - silence

"Dude?"

"Yeah?"

"I got an English exam in an hour."

"That oughta be interesting."

"Yeah."

And that's where I was when I looked over, saw my brain floating just to the left of my head, asking me if I had any idea what the prof was asking for in that essay.

Nah dude, you?

Not a clue.

Then get back in there where you belong before you get me in trouble.

I got a B for the semester anyway.

Better Home

He set his banjo on a peach crate,
picked up a mason jar,
tore himself off a slash and said,
"Sing for me, Vera."
Her voice wavered like a robin's song,
high and clear across the smoke-filled room
and everybody drew still as Grandma sang gospel.

"I was standing, by my window,
On one cold and cloudy day"

Grandaddy's fingers skipped across the banjo strings
like Mama through a Carolina cotton field,
bare feet kicking clods of red dirt
while her patchwork dress
snagged on branches,
snatchin' notes out of the air like
Grandma's song floating through the kitchen
while she fixed collards for Sunday dinner.

"Will the circle be unbroken,
By and by, Lord, by and by."

The whiskey stole his fingers,
hard living and twelve children stilled her voice.
There was no music in them
by the time I came along,
but every once in a while,
when I played freeze tag with my cousins
In the back yard and hid behind the laundry
hanging out in the sun to dry,
a bird would carry back a hint of melody, and I could
hear the song

in Grandma's eyes as she stood at the sink
washing dishes
and watching the kids play in the yard.

*"There's a better home a-waiting,
in the sky, lord, in the sky."*

The Christmas Lights

Every year, the day after Thanksgiving, when all the women were running around to the mall looking for the latest sale on this or that, Jeremiah Green would get up early, go to the garage and get down the cardboard boxes of lights. Then he'd get out the ladder, the hammer, and the extension cords and set to work. He'd work most of the day, with a break around lunchtime for a sandwich made from yesterday's dried-out turkey on white bread with French's yellow mustard and Miracle whip and maybe some celery on the side with salt sprinkled on it. He'd sit on the porch in his old flannel shirt eating his turkey sandwich and celery, and crack open a Pabst from the cooler in the garage.

Helen didn't cotton much to drinkin' so he only had a beer on those rare occasions when she was gone and he had the house to himself. Most years a six-pack bought after the Fourth of July would last the rest of the year, then he'd allow himself another beer or two for New Year's after Helen had gone to bed. She'd long since given up caring about watching some silly ball drop, figuring that she could tell it was a new year when she looked at the calendar the next morning at breakfast. The day changed every evening without her help; she didn't need to stay up past her bedtime just to ring anything in.

Jeremiah liked to watch all the commotion on the tv, so he usually stayed up and had himself a beer or two while that Clark fella nattered on until he fell asleep.

Then he'd wake up sometime in the middle of the night and go to bed.

Then once he finished his turkey sandwich, Jeremiah (not once in his eighty-two years was he ever Jerry or Jer, or God forbid, Jed) would lean the ladder up against the side of the house and start to string the lights. By the time Helen got home from shopping with her sisters it would be full-on dark, and Jeremiah would be back inside watching Wheel of Fortune or Jeopardy if she ran particularly late. Once she got home and got all her prizes deposited in the front bedroom for later wrapping and distribution, they'd go out in the front yard together and take a minute standing on the lawn of the house he bought when he got home from the war, a time he never really talked about, not even to Helen.

They'd admire his handiwork, Helen would remind him to put the ladder away before they went to bed, and he'd reply that it would get done eventually, and anyway, what if there was a light burnt out? Then he'd go up to the outlet he had installed on the porch by that Reynolds boy down the street just for this purpose, and he'd plug in the main extension cord.

With that, the whole front of the house, roofline, bushes, little cedar tree by the driveway and all the porch railings burst into white light, and the whole neighborhood could tell that the holidays were upon them. There were never any colored lights, at least not since 1973 when Jeremiah shaved off those sideburns. There were never any flashing lights or strobe lights, and never any plastic Santas and reindeer on the roof. There was just a bright white celebration of the season.

For over fifty years, from the time the armistice was signed and Jeremiah came home from Korea, he dragged that ladder out of the garage every November and lit up the night sky in a celebration of the season, of family, and of just being alive.

Until this year. When Helen passed in August Jeremiah sat down in that vinyl recliner in the den with a Pabst, probably the first time in thirty years he'd had a beer in August inside his house, and it seemed like he didn't move from that chair for months. Neighbors would come to visit, to see how he was holding up, and he'd tell them, in the stoic way of octogenarian men who've seen young men die, that he was doing about as well as could be expected.

As well as could be expected didn't really amount to much, he thought to himself after the well-wishers, the pastors and deacons, the neighborhood widows and friends of his children that had moved away years before and were back in town visiting their own parents had left. As well as could be expected was getting up three times in the middle of the night to pee and being confused every single time when he went back to bed and there was no one there. As well as could be expected was fixing his own breakfast every morning and finally going into the garage to drag out the old coffee pot that Helen had wanted to toss out twenty years ago when they got the new programmable kind but he wouldn't let her for fear that just this thing would someday happen and he'd have to make his own coffee and be too old and near-sighted to read the instructions on the damn thing and besides, what does a coffeepot need all them damn buttons for anyhow? You just put the coffee in it, put some hot water in it, and it turns into coffee. It doesn't need a clock in it, much less more buttons than one for off and one for on.

So as well as could be expected wasn't really very well at all, if he would take the time to think about it. Which he didn't, because Jeremiah was never a man to spend too much time in deep contemplation. But now, at 82, there wasn't a whole lot left for him to do except sit. And think. And since thinking was less appealing, he managed to lose himself in some of the seventy-six channels of eternal drivel that spouted from the 19" color television that sat in the living room on top of the old console tv that had finally breathed its last some eight years ago. So Jeremiah sat. And watched tv. And that's how most days went. He watched tv until bedtime, watched the late news and went to bed, where he lay awake listening to the silence beside him until sleep finally took him off for a couple of hours at a time.

So on this Friday after Thanksgiving, instead of listening to Helen get up at the crack of dawn to go shopping with her sisters, then getting up to drink the coffee she left for him in the machine he never did figure out how to operate, then heading out to the garage to start on the decorations, he sat. He turned on the tv and watched a little bit of that, then fixed himself a dry turkey sandwich with Miracle Whip from the leftovers from the turkey that the Methodist women brought by on Wednesday.

He ran out of mustard last week and kept forgetting to put it on the list that hung on the refrigerator. If he didn't write it down, he wouldn't remember to get it when he went grocery shopping this Sunday, either. He had taken to grocery shopping at eleven on Sundays so he didn't have to worry about seeing any of the church women in the store. Helen had always been real active in the church, but with her gone he didn't see much sense in him going. He figured he and God still had a few things they needed to sort out from about fifty years ago, but they were the sort of things a man needed to talk through with his maker face to face, and going to church wouldn't do him a whole lot of difference one way or the other.

As he was sitting, not really enjoying his mustardless sandwich but not really not liking it either, he started to hear some rattling around in his garage. The neighborhood, which had been full of young veterans when they moved in all these years ago, had seen its ups and downs, and was currently on the beginning of one of the up periods, which was to say that there were a lot more people living there at the moment who could be considered down than up, but in general they were hard-working people who didn't cause too much trouble. The people on the tv liked to talk about it as a neighborhood "in transition," but Jeremiah just thought that was a fancy way of saying there were some poor people that lived there, some white people, some black people and some Mexicans thrown in for good measure. There was some crime, sure, but in general it was decent place to live. But when he heard somebody rattling around in his garage, he didn't run out to go look and see what they might be stealing.

It's not that he was afraid that whoever was in his garage might hurt him. He'd known pain at different times in his life, you didn't make it past fourscore years on this earth without getting hurt more than once, but he just really wasn't that interested. And as the day wore on and the noise in his garage continued off and on, he finally decided that if there was something worth taking out there they should have already took it and left him alone, so he went to the back door and stuck his head out to yell at whatever hooligans were back there.

But by this time whatever perpetrators there had been were already gone, so all he saw was a closed garage door and a quiet back yard. He went back inside and dozed in front of his tv for the rest of the afternoon, watched a little football, not that he knew or cared anything about any of the schools playing, but it was something to pass the time, and napped a little more.

Along about seven o'clock, he started to listen for Helen's sister Mary's car, and then remembered that Mary didn't drive anymore after she got so blind they took her license away last summer, and besides, she wasn't going to be dropping Helen off tonight anyhow. But as he stood in his kitchen alone, feeling once again the lost feeling of someone who is missing something that he just can't quite put his finger on what it is, there was a knock at his front door. He had left all the porch lights off to keep folks from coming by to check on him since he didn't really feel like sharing another afternoon of how you holdin' ups with somebody who he didn't really give much of a damn about and he figured didn't give much of a damn about him either, so the knock was a little surprising. He figured it was a kid, since they weren't usually smart enough to figure out that when the porch light wasn't on it meant that the body inside didn't want to be bothered.

So he made his way through the darkened house to the front door, and pulled it open to find an empty porch. He looked around for a minute, confused, before he saw it laying over to the right of the door. It was an orange extension cord with a red bow tied to the end of it. On the bow was a card, and Jeremiah reached down and pulled the card off the end of the card and read it.

"Dear Mr. Jeremiah,
We are sorry that your wife died. We are sorry that you are sad, and that you didn't want to put your pretty lights up this year. We hope we did it good and it will make you a little happy.

Feliz Navidad,

Jose y Hector Garcia (from across the street)"

Jeremiah stood there for a minute looking around, not really knowing what to think, when he looked up and saw two boys looking out of a living room window across the street. The bigger one looked like he was about thirteen, and the little one looked to be maybe eight. The big one just watched him, but when the little one saw him looking, he waved excitedly, indicating that Jeremiah should plug in the cord.

So he did, and he walked out on his lawn to see his house lit up just like it was every year, with white lights on the little cedar tree by the driveway, on the porch railings, on all the bushes on the front of the house, and even on the roofline, although how those little boys got all the way up there he had no idea. Until he saw his ladder leaning up against the side of the house just like it did every year until after he got everything working just right. He stood there for a minute imagining he could feel a smaller hand in his own as he stood there on his lawn not quite as alone as he'd been a couple hours before, then he turned around, nodded to the two boys in the window, one waving like his arm was one a spring, and one nodding back solemnly, gathered his ladder, and put it away in his garage until after New Year's.

Gingham

Little girl standing by the railroad tracks
brown pigtails sticking out akimbo from her head
blue gingham dress
checked
with an apron that started life as white
before it went through three cousins
and one older sister.
Little girl standing all alone,
looking down the track and
wondering
When's Daddy comin' home?

Little girl sitting on the porch
gingham dress too short and threadbare,
knobby knees poking out
the first beginnings of bumps under her apron
just starting to swell and show.
still enough of a little girl to sit cross-legged on the
porch swing
waiting for big sister to come home
off her date with the Swain boy
who drives the loud car and smells like whiskey,
looks at her behind while she walks up the steps
telling little girl to go to bed
"you wouldn't act like this if Daddy was here."

Little girl walking across a stage,
flat cap on her head
hot June afternoon in a blue gown
grabs that piece of paper and
Looks
up in the stands

where sits a proud mama
big sister and her baby girl
and that Swain boy
who made a decent husband after all
but still a Daddy-shaped hole
in the air next to Mama.

Little girl sits on a porch
in a shapeless black dress
as aunts and uncles
and more cousins than you can shake a stick at
sit in the living room swapping memories and telling
lies
knees drawn up cross-legged under her on the porch
swing
again
sweet tea glass sweats untouched on the porch rail
with a slice of lemon on the rim
drawing flies
as she looks down the driveway
until at last an old man
looking uncomfortable in a shiny new suit
and never broken in shoes
limps past the rusted mailbox into view.

He stops at the gate,
takes off his hat,
looks at the little girl
and she looks back.
He nods,
she waves a shy little girl wave with half her hand
like she was six instead of twenty-six
and goes back inside the house
leaving the old man
at the end of the driveway
watching the tea glass sweat in the August dusk

Driving to See Mama

This is a story my father told me, in the best re-creation of his words I can devise. The year is 1950, the place is Camp Atterbury in Edinburgh, IN.

So this ol' boy Briggs come into the barracks one afternoon and says "Johnny Bob, you got any money? They're giving out three-day passes and we got a quart of liquor and a tank full of gas, but we ain't got enough money to get all the way to Asheville. If you got enough money to get a tank of gas in London, Kentucky, I can get more money in Asheville."

Now this was 'long about the end of the month when didn't nobody have no money, so I told him No.

"C'mon John, I know you always got a dollar or two ratted away, count up your change and see how much money you got."

Well, I did have a dollar or two stuck back, and I had two dollars in my pocket, and when I counted up all my change I had $5.30. We decided that was enough for a tank of gas, so off we went. We had us an Oldsmobile 88 convertible, and it was February, so we had the top up, and the windows rolled up, and as soon as we pulled out of the base, Briggs tore the top off that quart of liquor and threw it out the window.

Well, we got to London, Kentucky, and we filled up, and it cost us four dollars and a quarter for a tank of gas. Now I had $5.30, and that's all the money that was in that car. The other boys had done spent all their money on that quart of liquor and the first tank of gas. So we bought another quart of liquor, on credit, from that store in London.

Now I always did wonder why that ol' boy let us have that liquor on credit, but come to think of it, there was six of us, all of us big men, all of us MPs from Camp Atterbury, and all of us about half drunk. Hell, he mighta been a little scared!

But the funny part of the story is this - Briggs had it in his head that that Oldsmobile was the fastest thing ever been made. Now this road from London to Asheville would go from four lanes to two, then back to dual lane for a little while, then back down to two lanes. And we're clipping along right real good on one of these dual-lane parts when we saw lights in the rear view. I think they were red lights back then, but it don't matter, it was the police.

Well, Briggs said "What kind of car is that that thinks they can catch me?" We told him it was a Chevrolet, and that ended that. Briggs stepped on the gas and thought he was gone pull away from the police car. Well, that didn't work out so good, and the faster Briggs went in that Oldsmobile, the closer that Chevrolet got. I tell you, he couldn't get no farther apart from that police car than I am to you. Well, he kept going 'til he finally got scared, and said "I guess I gotta pull over."

Well, there was six of us in that car, and we'd been drinking and smoking cigarettes since we left base, so when Briggs rolled down that window, all that smoke just chimneyed up out of that window and that policeman had to jump back.

"Damn! Smells like y'all been brewing whiskey in there!"

Well, he made us all get out of the car, all six of us. And then - now Briggs was a big man, about 6'6",250 lbs. and he didn't have no gut on him. He was just broad through the shoulders, a big man. And Briggs, he just starts to sob, right there on the side of the road. And he's just weeping, and out he comes with this.

"I'm sorry officer, but my buddy Warren here's mama is dying and we're just trying to get him back to Asheville so he can say goodbye to his mama. We just gotta get him back to see his mama before she dies."

Now Warren was an orphan, and never knew he even had a mama, so this was all news to him! And that policeman thought about it for a minute and finally he said "I don't know if I oughta believe that sob story, but if I take you in and lock you up, and then I find out it is true, well then I'd feel like a real heel. So if you'll let the soberest one of you drive, I'll let you go."

Then he comes over to me, and says "I don't know if you're any more sober than they are, or if you just handle it better, but if I let you go, will you drive?"

I said "Yes sir, and I'll drive carefully." And damn if he didn't let us go!

Gold, Pop. Pure gold. He told me he's been telling that story for 57 years, and it's still funny. I agree.

My South *(A new redneck anthem)*

My South has a chip on its shoulder.

My South doesn't care how you did it up North.

My South does NOT talk funny! And no, we will not say "dawg" again just for your amusement!

My South is TIRED of y'all tryin' to sound Southern on TV, making jokes about Rednecks and still comin' down here every year cloggin' up our beaches and mountains.

My South gave you William Faulkner, Pat Conroy, Tennessee Williams AND Thomas Wolfe. Whattayou got?

My South invented NASCAR and you wish you did. My South is Dale Earnhardt #3 and #8. My south is Tobacco Road and Football Friday nights. My South is Dean Smith, Hank Aaron and WOOOOO! Ric Flair.

My South is Hank Williams 1, 2 AND 3. Toby Keith AND the Dixie Chicks. OutKast AND Earl Scruggs. My South is Stevie Ray Vaughan, Waylon Jennings and By God Johnny Cash will NEVER die as long as I'm still wearing black.

My South has attitude and a long memory. My South has learned from her mistakes. My South gave you

George Wallace AND Dr. King, and my South still has that dream.

My South is my daddy getting' up at 5 o'clock every morning, climbin' into a log truck and workin' like a dog past dark every night. At 75 years old. My South is still calling her "Mama" after all these years and not thinkin' nothing about it. My South is homemade peach ice cream, cookin' a pig for Fourth of July, cake walks at square dances and a mountain of casseroles after my brother's funeral, because my South takes care of her own.

My South is freeways AND Dirt roads. Pig pickin's AND gourmet cuisine. Merlefest AND Spoleto. My South revels in our contradictions and is never, EVER short on style.

And Give Me Back My Black T-Shirt

So I sat there, knees pulled up into my chest, long hair spilling down over my face, resting my head on my kneecaps. I was sitting in the pantry of our apartment on the floor, looking across the room at our Salvation Army dining room set, where a black felt box sat on a pink receipt, bright and cheerful. Mocking me.

I didn't even have a good song playing in the background. There wasn't any cool rotating jib pull-out to reveal the visual depths of my solitude. I didn't punch walls or flip over furniture or go into a good "Hulk Smash" routine where I pull a Van Halen and send my TV crashing into the parking lot one floor below. Too many bushes down there for a decent crash, anyway.

There was just me, and the fast beeping of the telephone telling me get up off my ass and hang up the phone. But I couldn't do it. Not only could I not move, but I couldn't think about hanging up the phone. Because that would be admitting it was over. That my idea of a perfect little life was down the shitter with one call.

It sucks getting dumped. It sucks more getting dumped via telephone. But I'm pretty sure I get some kind of prize for the level of suck involved in getting dumped via telephone by your fiancé's *best fucking friend* while aforementioned fiancé is off on another continent who calls in the middle of an otherwise perfectly lovely afternoon and said "Sherry called me. She told me to tell you not to buy the ring."

My roommate came home an indeterminate time later and found me in the pantry. She didn't say anything, just sat there in the pantry with me and held while I shook, cried, cursed and begged for answers. She didn't have any, either, except to say "I'm here."

Eventually I got up off the floor. Eventually I put all her shit in a box and when she got back from digging up relics in the Middle East for her summer internship I gave all her crap back to her on a lunch break from working a concert. Eventually I met someone else, fell in love and got married. Eventually I started to write again. Eventually I reconnected with some of what she ripped out of me, poured gasoline on, burned to a crisp and then salted the earth from where it sprung.

But that night, while I looked across my kitchen at the engagement ring I had bought for her that day, I couldn't see eventually. The world had gone monochrome for me, and I sat there remembering changing her tire for her after freshman Western Civ class, catching 3AM Taco Bell after sitting in the amphitheatre on campus talking until past 2AM on our first date, eating Little Debbie Star Crunches naked on my bed while her red hair trailed over her breasts like a modern day Godiva with ringlet curls. All those memories went from vibrant to sepia in a second while I felt something deep within me die.

Sunday Morning

I'm watching you sleep on a Sunday morning,
With the cat curled up on your feet, a calico ballast
as you oh-so-slightly snore into your pillow.
An errant curl snakes along your cheek,
Dances with freckles
Tickles your nose,
You twitch
The cat grumbles
I brush the hair back in place as the sun slowly
Crawls
Up your legs,
Warming the room as it makes its slow
Steady
Way
To breakfast.

Rainbow

After the lightning stopped
and the wind died down
I crawled out from under my hastily erected shelter
and picked up the pieces of my life
that your storm scattered across the world
for all my neighbors to see.
I walked around picking up broken feelings
and shattered memories,
mementoes from vacations that I thought meant
something
at the time.
I took the soggy pictures of you and me with Goofy
at Disneyworld
and I put them in a box
along with the mix tape I made you for your trip
(I thought it was a little cold to give that back to me)
and the sweatshirt that was really mine
but you liked it so much I thought of it as yours
and I packed it all away in my memory
and tried to forget the storms of you,
but the rainbow wouldn't let me

Salt

I can still taste the salt on your lips –
Sun-kissed blonde and sweet, sweet seventeen
Graduation week daquiris, sand surf
summer lovin'
tell me more
tell me Mooorrrree
Wave-tossed kisses
Under the Boardwalk
As the water licks our toes
You giggle.

I can still taste the salt on your lips –
Tangled clothes bare back sticking to the car seat
Elbows, knees and nothing fitting right
Ooooh, ow, no, yes, right theeerrrreeee
Shit, car's coming
Can't see to drive
Laughing, sweating, panting
growing up fast together
on an empty dirt road
Shirt on inside out walking in the front door
and Mama waiting in the kitchen

I can still taste the salt on your lips –
Feel your hair on the back of my hand
As the wind blows off the lake
You cling to me
One
last
time

And a single
Sweet
Salty
Tear
Runs down your face

Or mine.

3rd Thursday in November

1994, Saturday. Two days after Thanksgiving. Suzy and I have been together for a couple of months now and I'm spending pretty much every weekend at her place now, so that's where I'm found. It's late-ish, maybe 11. Far enough into the evening that when my pager goes off, it's a little unusual. When the phone rings downstairs, we ignore it, because it's Saturday night and we're doing what young couples do on Saturday nights when their relationship is new. Think back, you'll remember.

When the cell phone rings and the pager goes off again, I'm perplexed enough to answer my cell. It's John Fore, one of my roommates from Rock Vegas.

"Yeah, what?" somewhat annoyed.

"Dude. Call your Dad. He's trying to find you."

"What's up?" becoming concerned, because my Dad never calls. Anyone.

"I dunno, he just told me to have you call home."

Hang up, scared now. I look at my pager, it's my parent's number. Seriously concerned now, I go downstairs to hear my dad leaving a message on the machine

"...call me as soon as you get this, it's important."

I pick up, dial him back.

"Hey. What's wrong?" In my parent's world, nobody ever calls anyone after 9PM unless something is terribly wrong.

There's a pause, and I know it's bad.

"Wayne was killed in a car wreck a little while ago."

"No."

Beat.

"What happened?"

"We don't know yet."

"Should I come home?"

"No. There's nothing you can do tonight. Come home tomorrow morning, we'll know more then."

Beat.

"I need to go, I still have to call Bobby."

"Alright. I'll see you tomorrow."

And as I curl up into a ball, naked under the bar in my condo's kitchen, cold linoleum slowly imprinting flower patterns onto my legs and side, I realize that my brother is gone. Just like that, with a phone call, shit has become seriously fucked up.

Wayne was my brother-in-law. He married my sister

Bonnie when I was a year old. I am the youngest of four children, current ages 56, 53, 52 and 36. So there's a little bit of a disconnect there. Until I got out of college, my siblings had always been more like other sets of parents or aunts and uncles than brothers and sisters. And I was always closest to Bonnie and Wayne.

Bonnie wanted to have kids in the absolute worst way, and it was a long time in coming for her, so she took me in as my second mom before I was out of Mama's arms. I spent as much of my waking time at her house as I did my own when I was a kid, and their friends Ginny, Herb, Cranford and Lana and Joe were my extended family too. When Jessica and Stephanie were born, she had her own kids to raise, but as we've grown older, we've grown closer, and today she's my running buddy, my musical partner in crime and the person I'm probably most likely to end up drunk in a ditch with. You could say we're close.

So to have Wayne ripped away from us that quickly was absolutely fucking devastating. I have never experienced anything quite so suddenly shattering, not even when my fiance dumped me from across the Atlantic Ocean.

You'd never know it to look at him, but my father is an incredibly softhearted man. He's a slightly gnarled sunburnt stump of a man with woodcutter arms and a plodding half-stomp of a gait, but he taught me that it's okay for a man to cry. We watched MASH together and wept like little girls when Henry Blake's chopper got shot down. So it wasn't a huge surprise to see him crying outside my sister's house when I walked onto her porch. But I had never seen my brother Bob cry before. But Bobby was crying too that day, and it broke my shit right up. I remember only snapshots from those next few days -

My sister sitting on the couch looking for all the world like someone in advanced Alzheimer's, just uncomprehending. The epitome of the word "haunted eyes."

Walking down the hallway that Monday in the theatre building at school and finding Marc, the chair of our department to tell him that I wouldn't be in classes for a few days, could he make that all work out for me, and this 6' 3" bear of a guy just folding me into a hug that for a second at least, held my pain at bay and let me feel safe.

The amazing amount of food spread through every room of Bonnie's double-wide. Southerners understand that not only is the way to win a heart through the stomach, but often the way to heal one begins there as well. The people of that small community made sure that my whole family's physical comforts were taken care of for those days while we tried to begin to patch our hearts together.

Standing outside the funeral home waiting for Bonnie to get there so we could all have one moment together before the flood of people started through. Bonnie has never been considered the most timely of people, and she took a little longer getting there than the rest of us. My niece Dianne, Bobby and I were standing out back waiting for her when Bobby said "Well, we always said she'd be late for her own funeral. I guess this is as close as you can really get."

Mama slapped his arm, and I laughed for the first time in three days.

I don't remember much of the funeral. Nothing of what was said. Those aren't the things that stand out at those moments. I remember Danny Wallace's ponytail. I remember the sadness in Robert Blair's eyes. I remember people hugging me that I hadn't seen in years. I remember Mike Wallace and I talking for the first time in years.

So this is a holiday for giving thanks. Really. Take a minute and look around the table, and be fucking thankful, because it can all change too fast. I still remember the conversations we had that Thanksgiving, because we were all talking about how much Wayne's hair looked like Toby Keith's mullet, and how that boy was never gonna have a hit if he didn't fix that hair.

Destination Anywhere

Where you going, little brown haired girl,
In your white cargo pants slung low enough on your
hips
That I can see your Hello Kitty thong?
I see you solemn,
Leaning against the signpost at the bus stop
Waiting on the number 7 get me the hell outta here
line
With one earbud hanging down across your
collarbone
Poking out of your pink wifebeater
And the other in your ear,
Playing cat and mouse with your dirty blonde hair,
KT Tunstall singing something about black horses
and cherry trees.
You're digging your toes in the grass
As a pair of worn-out flip-flops dangles from one
hand
And your eyes stare off
At a tomorrow that never comes
No matter how fast you chase it.

Crying in the Rain

The funny things about crying in the rain
is that you can't tell which is which.
I'm sitting on the porch
under an overflowing gutter
with a clogged downspout
as a sheet of water pours over me,
late-summer thunderstorm washing away
the mourning.
A miserable yellow dog slinks down the sidewalk
giving me an incredulous look and shake of the head.
I hear the intermittent chirp of a baffled bluejay
interspersed with the splatter, splatter of raindrops on
asphalt.
The occasional sound of patent leather through mud
puddles
tells the story of comings
and goings
from the house behind me.
I hate the rain,
but I hate being in there more
dodging platitudes and sandwich platters,
and if I see one more goddamn broccoli casserole
I think I'm gonna shoot somebody.

Anniversary in Italy

"This is the best swordfish steak I have ever tasted." I said to the maitre'd. He was hovering since we were the first couple in for the dinner hours.

"Thank you, I will tell my uncle you enjoyed it."

"Is he the chef?"

"No, he is a fisherman. He caught that fish this morning."

This conversation simply does not happen in North Carolina. For one thing, all the grammar was too good. But since I wasn't in North Carolina, rather Taormina, Sicily, I didn't think too much of the statement. It was our anniversary, and we had ditched the tour group to do a little shopping and have a nice romantic dinner all to ourselves. So we meandered the cobblestone streets of Taormina, wandered through the piazza centro and set off down a side street where I noticed a small sandwich board in front of a lighted canopy.

"Let's try this place."

"Okay, whatever you want."

"Happy anniversary."

"Happy anniversary. So where are we going next year?"

"Let's just see if they have seats first, then we can think about next year."

They did have seats, since it was only 7PM and barely the beginning of dinner hours. I love the idea of a siesta, the nap in the midday that allows everything to be postponed a little into the evening. After all, only mad dogs and Englishmen go out in the midday sun. And Americans, but that's beside the point. The point is, 7PM was very early for dinner, so we had the restaurant all to ourselves for our anniversary dinner, from the antipasti all the way to the tiramisu, which after that meal I simply refuse to eat anywhere on American soil. It's simply a pale reflection.

The prosciutto was fresh, and sliced thin enough to be pinkly translucent. The wine was exquisite, a light and airy Aetna white, so named because the vineyard was on the slopes of that great smoking mountain where we had spent the previous day exploring. For a pasta, I chose spaghetti with sea urchin, tiny balls of sea urchin meat the size of the end of a Q-tip, with a flavor that exploded across the mouth and tongue like a rich, salty firecracker. An oddly earthy taste, sea urchin, brought out well by the slight dusting of Parmesan cheese (Suzy had made the tactical error on our first afternoon of assuming that Parmesan cheese in Sicily was as milquetoast and bland as the Americanized green cardboard can version. Not even close.)

And then there was the grilled swordfish, which I ate without the slightest interest in overfishing, endangered species, or anything else except the fever

pitch my tastebuds had been brought to by this meal.
Light and flaky, but not dry. Exquisitely seasoned,
with herbs and sea salt, the fish was substantial
enough to rival any NY strip steak I've ever eaten,
without the sense of substance. It was filling, yet after
the meal was finished I felt almost as though I had
dined on moonlight and rainwater. There was nothing
to weigh us down as we thanked the nice man for his
hospitality, took a photo with him for our scrapbook,
and wandered back down the cobblestone alley into
the night.

Independence Blvd. Evening

I'm driving in the rain with my sunglasses on,
watching the wipers slap time with my iPod
as I cruise on searching for a rainbow
or at least a pot of gold
or maybe a little pot.
A gnarled white-haired black man in a trench coat
holding an umbrella
hops a Jersey barrier as he meanders across
eight lanes of 7 o'clock traffic
slipping across the mix of oil and water
making a mother-of-pearl sheen on black.
Bridge ices before road
Slippery when wet
Caution men working
End construction – a protest sign
and we all dodge the state tree of North Carolina -
the orange road cone –
as the soundtrack of our cages runs us ragged on
home

Fugue in Geek Minor

I was 18 years old and full of my own independence. Jason, Steve and I had torn off down to New Orleans for Fall Break, gotten drunk at Wet Willie's, pissed in a public park under a streetlight and gotten front row seats at Big Daddy's Topless & Bottomless, where a Eurasian chick with a black pageboy cut and three tattoos did things to Jason's hat that made him swear he would never do laundry again. So when the chance came up to go to Dragon Con that year, I was totally there.

I'd never done a major Con before, and Dragon Con was pretty damn major. I found out that Todd McFarlane was going to be there, so I packed up my Spiderman #1 in my backpack, tossed a bottle of Mescal under the front seat of my 1978 Impala, and we cruised off down I-85. Steve was originally from G-Vegas, and we were meeting up with Jay and a bunch of his friends from the Greenville Rogues Society, who threw an annual party at Dragon Con that was apparently something not to be missed.

Hell, the whole trip was something not to be missed. From drinking White Russians with Jay that had so much liquor in them they actually fermented the milk, to seeing the bodies lying in the hallway of the Atlanta Hilton (I think) sprawled on the floor, mouths agape with black drool dribbling down their chin after drinking The Black Death (a Rogues Society Specialty), the whole weekend was incredible. It can all be summed up for me by one brief moment.

We were in a ballroom waiting for the dance to start, but there was no music. We'd had about a gallon of White Russians at this point and I felt the need to lie down. As I lay there, I noticed that the chandelier in the room was really neat-looking from that angle, so I called over Jay's friend Carol, who also was feeling a bit of a need to be recumbent just about then. So Carol and I lay in the center of the ballroom exploring the landscape of the chandelier when I felt a twinge in my neck.

I turned my head ever so slightly to notice that there was someone biting me. A smallish woman, at least from what I could tell given the relative angles, with tricolor hair. Platinum, red and goth black. She nibbled a little longer, then she kissed me. Rather intently. I decided this couldn't be all bad, so I kissed her back and nibbled a little on her neck in return. After a couple of nips and nibbles, she suggested we depart the ballroom for somewhere a little more private.

I thought briefly of going off to have wild gymnastic monkey sex with a woman with whom I had yet to actually meet and who introduced herself to me, if you could call it that, by getting down on her hands and knees in the middle of a hotel ballroom floor and biting me on the neck, but then I decided I was really drunk and should get a second opinion.

"Carol, should I go fuck her?"

"No, honey, that would not be good."

"Sorry, my friend says I shouldn't go fuck you. But

thanks."

"Thanks, Carol."

"Friends don't let friends fuck dogs, baby."

I saw the tricolor-hair vampiress the next day. I wept a little as I thanked Carol from the bottom of my little bitty heart, because while she didn't have the kind of beauty that makes time stand still, she certainly had a face that could stop a clock.

Blues

The Chickasaw Mud Puppies twang my off-key
memory as road winds up behind me like video tape
on a proud papa's Super 8 handheld.

Xerox towns flicker past, the same fat bald men
playing checkers and talking politics as they sip from
a Ball jar in the shade while lavender-rinsed
socialites shop for gossip and cantaloupe at the
Piggly Wiggly.

I roll up and idle my engine at the lone blinking
caution light and listen –

While the mournful strains of Red River Valley
pierces pure the veil of heat and hypocrisy that hangs
over the town like a down comforter in the middle of
August.

On the porch of an unpainted shotgun shack, an old
black man with pepper-shaker hair
And lightning-bolt eyes
Blows harp.

The harmonica is a gymnast in those calloused hand
with sausage fingers, knuckles like cypress roots
dance as the moan, moan of a 'Bama-bound train
Slips through whiskeyed lips.

I flip him a silver dollar, and take from him more
than I gave.

A Little Shelter

It was a little after ten when she walked in. Dad was wiping down the desk, and I was emptying out the spittoons. She was tall, attractive in a careworn manner, and alone.

"Can I help you ma'am?"

"I need a room for the night. Are there any available?"

"I'm sorry ma'am, we're full up."

"Miss."

"Pardon?"

"It's Miss. Not Ma'am. I'm no longer married."

"I see."

"No, I doubt that you do. But I don't mind."

"Well,…Miss, we don't have any rooms here, so maybe you…"

At that, Dad came around the desk, and stopped me.

"Would you like to have a seat, miss?"

"Yes, thanks you."

"David, move some of your things into my room for the night. We'll be bunking together."

"But… we don't even know this…"

"David."

He didn't need to add anything. At 35 years old, I still jumped whenever that old man said "Frog," and probably always would. When I came back downstairs, he and the woman were deep in conversation. They looked up when I came into the room, not like they'd been doing anything wrong, exactly. More like they had been sharing something that I wasn't going to be part of no matter how much explanation I received.
After I showed her to her (my) room, I went to Dad's room, and stretched out on the pallet I'd made up on the floor.

"Why did you let her stay?"

"Son, she's got nothing left. Her husband was killed in the War, and she tried to keep the place he'd made for them. She couldn't, and now she's running back to Mama and Daddy Back East, like she swore she'd never do. She's given up her life, her pride, and everything she's known. If I can give her back a little touch of something by letting her sleep here for one night, then that's the least I can do."

"She told you all that while I was upstairs."

"No, she didn't tell me any of that. I knew it the second I looked up across the room at her; saw that ring on her left hand, and that empty look in her eyes.

Maybe when you've spent 30 years watching people check in here on their way up, down and sideways through life, you'll see it too."

I stood behind that desk for another 40 years, but I never did.

Pecan Pie

Sitting at a bare table
in a sunny kitchen
while the weather contradicts everything.
I'm crying in my pecan pie
while I taste you in every bite
as the blue-haired DAR matrons
murmur appropriate nothings
in the parlor
and run their slightly disapproving white-gloved
fingertips
along the tops of the picture frames on the mantel.
All I want to do is scream
but all I do is sit there smelling your cooking
Wwhile I eat the last pie you baked for me.
I can almost hear the shuffle of your bedroom
slippers
on the cracked linoleum,
almost taste your pork chops and gravy
while I try to be nice
and not notice them
eyeballing your grandaddy's clock on the mantel.

It Wasn't Gas

appendagitis (ap·pen·da·gi·tis) inflammation of an
appendage, particularly of the epiploic appendages.
epiploic a. inflammation of one or more of the
epiploic appendages of the colon, characterized by
pain and tenderness over the affected area.

In English, it's the inflammation of a fatty pocket that
is attached to the colon. In practice, it's 7 hours in the
emergency room, a CT scan of my most impressive
body part (unfortunately, my gut), injection of iodine
dye into my left arm after failing miserably to find a
vein in my right hand (proving that I would make a
terrible smack junkie, crossing off one of the careers
that a degree in acting left me perfectly trained for),
ingestion of a half-gallon of some type of lemonade-
flavored contrast solution, two courses of antibiotics,
and a bottle of hydrocodone that I'm thoroughly
enjoying.

I thought it was gas. I was on the road Wednesday,
and had a late lunch, which always leaves me a little
pooty. I was a little confused when my gut still hurt
Thursday morning, but figured maybe I had a fart
stuck somewhere and once I got to moving along, I'd
pass a good three-octave window-rattler and I'd be
fine.

When I stood up after lunch and almost fell down
from the pain I figured it might be something a little
more serious. Given the location of the pain (left side,
right along the beltline), I thought maybe a hernia.
That didn't make much sense, since the heaviest

thing I lift on a regular basis is my ass, but stranger things have happened I suppose. So I called my doctor.

"I'm sorry, we don't have any doctors in the office this afternoon."

Huh? It's 1:15 on a Thursday, and the Wachovia Championship was two weeks ago, so I can't imagine what important golf outing has them tied up. Not to mention the fact that my doctor is spherical in shape, which always makes me laugh when she tells me I'm overweight. She doesn't see the humor. Odd.

"So what am I supposed to do?"

"You can go to urgent care or to the emergency room."

I wasn't really looking forward to the concept of the emergency room, as I didn't want to hang with the dregs and the near-dead, so I trundled my sore ass (gut, actually) off to the urgent care facility in the yuppie part of town. They were very helpful, telling me that to diagnose severe abdominal pain it would require either an ultrasound or a CT scan, neither of which they could perform. So I should go to the emergency room. Well, fuck.

So I did, and was immediately triaged and put into the queue, leading to a three-hour wait while I watch some Mexican construction worker with a scratch on his forehead come in after me and get seen before me, a 923-year-old woman almost wet herself waiting for her ride back to the nursing home before she can convince someone to take her to the pisser,

Gilbert Grape's mother trundle in riding an overworked wheelchair with a trashcan in her lap for more convenient puking telling everyone that she's suicidal and thinks she's OD'd on her Xanax. This doesn't make sense to me, since if you OD on your antidepressant shouldn't you just be annoyingly perky? But who am I to question the collected wisdom of what is obviously 8 generations of trailer park education?

Then there was Tracy. I call her this because she looked a little like Tracy Chapman after a 9-year dessert bender, and to refer to her with anything resembling Buckwheat references would probably be deemed racist, regardless of the fact that she really did look like what happens when Buckwheat's kid sister grows up, and in a greater case, grows outward. Tracy walked up to the check-in station, picked up a pen to sign in at the desk, and immediately passed out sideways in a building-jarring thump (and kind of a wet slapping sound, like a 200-lb uncooked pork tenderloin hitting the tile) leaving one Wal-Mart sandal looking forlorn in front of the check-in station.

I leaned over to Suzy and said "I think I just got bumped one spot down in the treatment line."

After three hours of watching the very old, the very underinsured and the egregiously stupid traipse through the ER, it was my turn. Went back, put on my little gown (which they do apparently make in size Xfatass), and laid down on the less-than-comfortable stretcher. I had the foresight to bring a book, having spent far more of 2006 in a hospital than I care for, and Suzy was there for chat and to serve as my remote control.

I caught part of Sportscenter, and then Dr. Fratboy was in to see me. Dr. Rollin Fuller, MD was a very nice guy who with a first name like Rollin probably got the shit beat out of him a lot in 8th grade.

So Dr. Fuller thought it might be diverticulitis, based on the position of the pain, and scheduled a CT scan. So then cute Nurse Lisa came in to try (and fail miserably, thus ending my dreams of ever being as slim as Kate Moss) to find an easy vein in my right arm, then the left. We got the IV going, I got a shot of happy juice, and then it was more Sportscenter until my ride down to Radiology. We got in line behind a hi-tech bed with three drivers, hanging bags of clear shit, green shit and brown shit, all dripping into Methuselah's grandma. I told Ashando, my chauffer that she could go first, as it looked like she was a little more fucked up than me.

After an interminable time waiting, made much more pleasurable by the drugs now coursing through my system, I got stuck in the little tube, zapped through with whatever they zap you with, and eventually Dr. Frat Boy came back to tell me that I had a condition that I immediately went home to look up. And whattaya know? It wasn't gas after all.

Thanks for stopping by. Feel free to let me know if you liked it, hated it or just bought it out of pity. You can find me at www.johnhartness.com

www.ingramcontent.com/pod-product-compliance
Lightning Source LLC
Chambersburg PA
CBHW031901170626
46807CB00004B/1832